P9-EFI-829

Star Bright

To Min O'Brien,
my youngest angel
–A. M.

To Hazel
and Keith Reynolds,
my guiding stars
–P. H. R.

ATHENEUM BOOKS FOR YOUNG READERS
An imprint of Simon & Schuster Children's Publishing Division
1230 Avenue of the Americas, New York, New York 10020
Text copyright © 2014 by Alison McGhee
Illustrations copyright © 2014 by Peter H. Reynolds
All rights reserved, including the right of reproduction in whole or in part in any form.
ATHENEUM BOOKS FOR YOUNG READERS is a registered trademark of Simon & Schuster, Inc.
Atheneum logo is a trademark of Simon & Schuster, Inc.
For information about special discounts for bulk purchases, please contact Simon & Schuster Special Sales at
1-866-506-1949 or business@simonandschuster.com.
The Simon & Schuster Speakers Bureau can bring authors to your live event. For more information or to
book an event, contact the Simon & Schuster Speakers Bureau at 1-866-248-3049 or visit our website at
www.simonspeakers.com.
Reynolds Studio supervision by Julia Anne Young
Book design by Ann Bobco
The text for this book is set in Boswell.
The illustrations for this book are rendered in pen, ink, and watercolor and then digitally enhanced.
Manufactured in China
0714 SCP
First Edition
10 9 8 7 6 5 4 3 2 1
Library of Congress Cataloging-in-Publication Data
McGhee, Alison, 1960–
Star bright: a Christmas story / by Alison McGhee and Peter H. Reynolds. — First edition.
pages cm
Summary: "What can a small angel give a most important baby? A Christmas story about the greatest gift of all"—
Provided by publisher.
ISBN 978-1-4169-5858-1
ISBN 978-1-4424-7714-8 (eBook)
1. Jesus Christ—Nativity—Fiction. [1. Jesus Christ—Nativity—Fiction. 2. Christmas—Fiction. 3. Angels—
Fiction. 4. Gifts—Fiction. 5. Stars—Fiction.] I. Reynolds, Peter H., 1961– illustrator. II. Title.
PZ7.M4784675St 2014
[E]—dc23   2014008465

Alison McGhee
AND
Peter H. Reynolds

A CHRISTMAS STORY

Star
Bright

A
atheneum

Atheneum Books for Young Readers
New York   London   Toronto   Sydney   New Delhi

It was the end of December,
and a baby was soon to be born.

A baby!

In the heavens,   angels turned light with joy.

On Earth, travelers prepared gifts.

Gifts for the baby!

The newest angel watched   and wondered.

She too wanted to give the baby a gift.
She tried to think of things
that the baby might like.

Wind?

Wind to blow through the baby's hair.
Wind to make the flowers dance.

But wind was the gift of the sky.

Rain?

Rain to cool the baby's skin.

Rain to fill the puddles.

But rain was the gift of the clouds.

What about . . . music?

Music to make the baby laugh.
Music to sing the baby to sleep.

But music was the gift
of the songbirds.

The newest angel looked up.
The universe felt so big.
And she felt so small.

The newest angel looked down.
How vast the night sky was, and how dark.

All that darkness made her feel even smaller.
And a little lonely.
Babies were so small. . . .
Would the baby feel lonely too?

And then, far below, she saw others.

They too looked lonely—
No, they looked lost!

And then she knew.
She knew exactly what to give the baby.

She closed her eyes.

And she fluttered down—

tumbling,

floating,

drifting

down

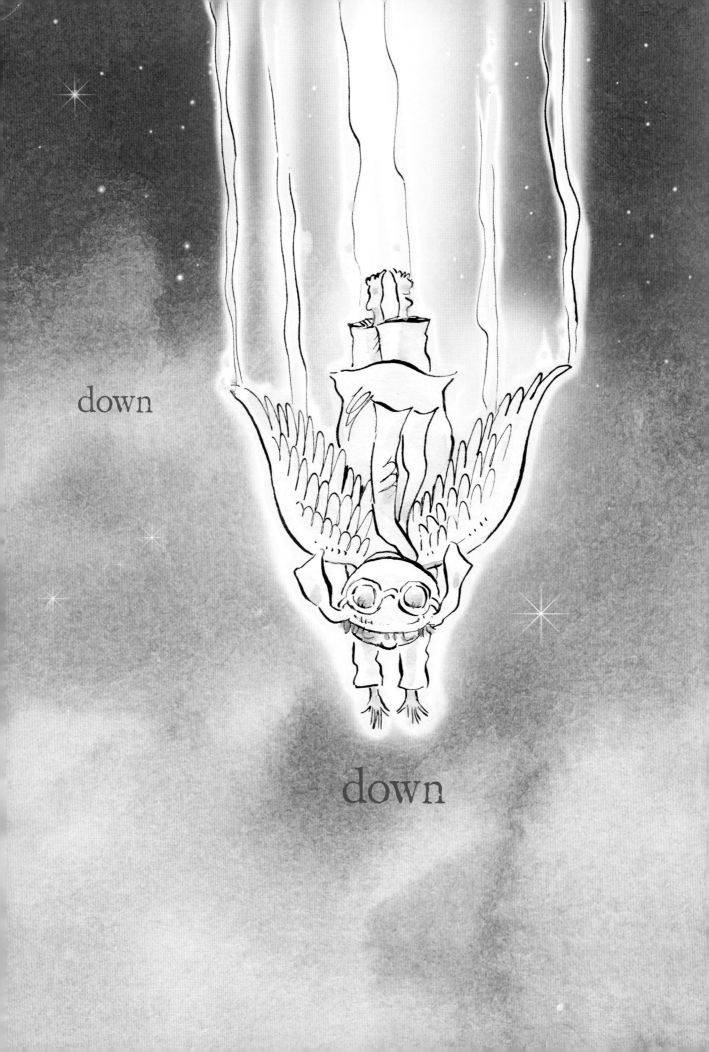

down

down.

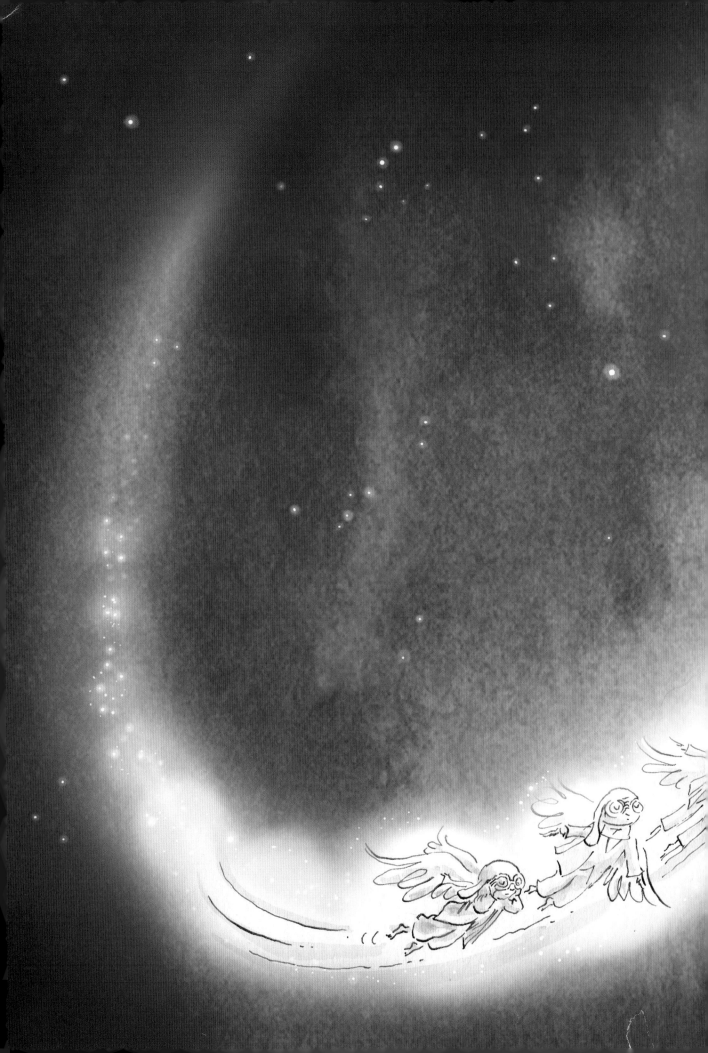

Until she came to rest exactly
where she was needed.

In the still of the night, the baby was born.
He opened his eyes to kind faces,
quiet animals, a soft blanket . . .

and a dark sky made
lovely with light.

Light in the darkness—
the best gift of all.